A POSY
POI

G000141273

Cara Louise

Chapter 1

"...and, although many people have kept watch at the crossroads over the years, no one has ever discovered who puts the flowers on Poll Moll's grave." Miss Tyler closed the book. There was silence in the class. Belinda leaned her elbow on the desk. It wasn't often l0a kept quiet.

"So that's what this year's play is about," said Miss Tyler. "As most of you know,every Halloween we put on a performance for the village. We have a long tradition of excellence and I'm sure this year we'll keep up the same high standards."

"Miss! Miss!" Belinda looked round as beside her, Susi Kettering shot up her hand and strained out of her chair. Susi was the only one who'd gone out of her way to be Belinda's friend. The rest of the girls had all been in school together since the first year - and didn't they let Belinda know it.

"Can I be Polly, Miss Tyler?" said Susie "Oh please, Miss?"

"You?" sneered Kim Maglione, from the back. "You're too fat!"

"Yeah," said Candice Smith, from her usual place beside Kim. "Polly was beautiful with long dark hair. Not a roly poly munchkin with hair like a toilet brush."

Belinda glanced at Susi and saw her cheeks were scarlet behind the straggly curtain of fair hair.

"That's enough," said Miss Tyler. "You'll all have the chance. In fact I expect to see all of you at the audition. I want a good show of support, seeing as I'm your form tutor."

Belinda's heart sank. She had only been attending Castle High for a fortnight. Her Dad's new job had taken them from London to Essex and she had left all her old friends behind.

This was the first she had heard about the school play, or Polly Miles. It was an interesting story, but the last thing she wanted was to be stuck up on a stage with everyone staring at her. It was bad enough being the new girl in school. She just wanted to blend in with the rest.

"Now," continued Miss Tyler. "I've chosen the story of Polly Miles, or Poll Moll, as she's sometimes called, because I thought it would be rather nice to do a local legend."

"Can't we do Dirty Dancing?" called Kim.

A titter went round the class.

Miss Tyler ignored it. "The first of November, the day after Halloween, is the anniversary of Polly's death, so it's quite fitting really."

"Susi could be a Halloween ghoul," sniggered Candice.

"That's enough!" Miss Tyler glared. Keep your eyes on the drama notice board. I'll be putting up a list of parts and times for the audition."

The sound of the bell ricocheted through the classroom. Miss Tyler picked up her books. "OK. Class dismissed. And go quietly!"

Chairs scraped against the floor and a hubbub of noise broke out, as 10a shovelled books and pencil cases into their bags then surged out of the classroom.

"I hate Kim and Candice," muttered Susi.

"It's best to ignore people like that," said Belinda, as they went into the corridor. "I bet neither of them get a part in the play. At least Miss Tyler knows you're keen."

"Do you think I stand a chance?" Susi brightened.

"'Course. Miss Tyler said everyone could audition."

"I wish I looked like you," sighed Susie "With all that long dark hair and your pretty face, then I might stand a chance."

"Don't be daft." Belinda looked down at the floor.

"I'm not. All the boys fancy you."

"No, they don't."

"Yes, they do. I've heard them."

Belinda blushed. "Is it good, the school play?"

"Brilliant. Last year we did "Robin Hood. I was one of the archers. Miss Tyler's a very good director and loads of people come to watch."

"Not to watch you, stumpy," said Kim, across her shoulder. "Or maybe they all came because they'd heard what a scream you looked, with your legs bulging out in green tights."

"Miss Tyler'll have to choose someone with long hair for Poll."

Susi scowled.

"Not necessarily, said "Belinda." Whoever she chooses could wear a wig."

"Yeah." Susi looked at her gratefully.

"It's more important to be a good actress," said Belinda.

Kim turned round. Candice stopped too, the pair of them blocking the corridor. Kim's eyes narrowed.

Belinda felt her heartbeat quicken. Her fingers gripped tighter around the strap of her bag. Kim reminded her of a cat she saw once, waiting beside a mouse hole.

"Just watch it, newbie," said Candice, brave beside Kim.

Belinda swallowed, but stood her ground.

Kim stepped very close and sneered, too close to her face. "Just be careful who you upset."

Kim and Candice paused, menacingly then turned and walked out of the door.

S usi scowled through the glass as Kim and Candice headed for the football pitch. "That Kim thinks she's God's gift."

"I wonder where they're off to," said Belinda. "We haven't got sports next."

"Kim's off to watch the boys playing footie," laughed Susie "So she can drool over Steve Winters' legs. Pathetic or what ?" I'

"Who's Steve Winters?"

"Captain of the football team."

"Does she fancy him?"

"Fancy him? Is the Pope a catholic? Most of the girls in this school fancy Steve Winters. He's gorgeous," sighed Susi. "Not that he'd look twice at me."

"You shouldn't put yourself down so much," said Belinda. "Anyway, it would be one in the eye for Kim if you got the part of Poll."

Susi grinned. "Yeah, it would. Come on, let's raid the chocolate machine."

Belinda made her way home through the village. It had not been a bad day, she thought to herself. The story about Poll Moll had been interesting and everyone was very excited about the play. Except her. But kids round here probably didn't get much to excite them, she thought, passing a row of little thatched cottages.

It was not at all like where she used to live in London, where there were cinemas, arcades and an ice rink. And a skateboarding park, and rollerblade ramps. She sighed as she remembered her old home. It was so different here. So quiet. She missed her friends. She was an outsider here. Susi was the only friend she'd made.

As she reached the end of the road, the ruinous walls of the old castle loomed up out of the park, reminding her of the story Miss Tyler had read.

What had happened that fateful 1st November, all those years ago? she wondered. How did Polly Miles vanish, on the night of the Samhain ball?

She continued through the village past the churchyard.

Something moved among the graves.

She stopped and looked across the wall.

Someone was watching her.

A young man, sturdily built, his hair flopping across his eyes, dug his spade into the ground and threw a shovelful of earth behind him. He continued to dig, but his eyes never left Belinda's face.

She looked away and tried to walk faster, without showing she was nervous. The sound of the spade crunched behind her, but as Belinda continued down the road, she could feel his eyes, staring at her still.

The wind snatched at her hair as she walked past the castle ruins in the park. From a clump of chestnut trees came the sound of children singing.

"Polly put the kettle on, Polly put the kettle on, Polly put the kettle on, We'll all have tea."

As she drew near the trees, the voices died away.

She glanced through the chestnuts, expecting to see the group of children playing beneath the autumn leaves.

She stopped abruptly. Around the park, trees were swaying in the wind, but on the chestnuts not a leaf stirred.

It was cold here, so cold.

But what really made her shiver was the empty space beneath the trees.

There was not a child in sight.

Chapter 2

"Oh great!" Susi pointed excitedly to the notice board outside the Hall. "The lists for the play must be up." She jostled to get through the group of drama hopefuls clustered around the board.

"3.45 Thursday, that's the first audition time," she stabbed the sheet of paper with a chubby forefinger. "Oh I really hope I get the part of Poll."

"You're too fat," came a voice behind them, and it was their turn to be jostled aside as Candice pushed her way to the front, followed by Kim.

"You mind your mouth," muttered Susi crossly. "Or..."

"Or what?" sneered Candice.

"Hey, 3.45 Thursday," said Kim. "I can just see myself as Poll."

"Come on," said Susi. "Let's go. There's a bad smell around here suddenly."

"Well, it looks like you'll have some competition for the lead role," said Belinda, as they headed away down the corridor. "Half the people round that board wanted the part of Poll."

"Oh I really hope I get it," said Susi, hugging her exercise books to her. "Kim and

Candice don't stand a chance. They auditioned last year and both of them have as much acting ability as a pudding. How about you, Bel? Are you going to audition for anything? There're loads of parts, all the village girls."

"Oh, I don't think so," said Belinda. "I've never done any acting. Not my thing, really. I don't fancy getting up on a stage with everyone staring at you."

"You'll come along and watch me audition though, won't you?" said Susi eagerly. "And it'll be a laugh. watching Kim and Candice making idiots of themselves."

"Yeah, okay," agreed Belinda. "I'll come along. I'll keep my fingers crossed you get to play Poll."

"Great," said Susie "Wow! I can hardly wait till Thursday."

"Right, who's here to audition as Sukey?" asked Miss Tyler, looking up from her clipboard across the drama studio. A few people put their hands up and she wrote down their names. "And Polly?" A sea of hands went up.

"There're plenty of other parts as well," Miss Tyler reminded them. "Some good character roles. Not everyone can play the lead."

She finished writing down the names of the people who had turned up for the audition then called the first ones up.

"Right," she said, handing out scripts. "We'll take the scene where Polly and her best friend Sukey are harassed by the jealous village girls for the attention paid to Poll by the Lord of the Manor's son. Page 12 of your scripts. Can everyone else sit down and keep quiet, please? Right, ready?"

The scene was repeated several times until most people had taken their turn at different roles. Susi's name was one of the last on the list. Many people had already gone home by the time Miss Tyler called her up to play Poll.

"Right, " said Miss Tyler, looking up from the clipboard. "I need someone to play spiteful Maggie Riley. Any volunteers?"

The only people left in the studio had already been allotted roles. The others had gone home, apart from Belinda who sat quietly watching at the back.

"We need someone," said Miss Tyler. "Isn't there anyone left? Ah, Belinda. Would you like to have a go?"

"Me?" Belinda felt her throat turn dry. "I... I'm only here to watch, Miss Tyler."

"We do need a Maggie," smiled Miss Tyler. "You'd really be helping us out."

"Well, I suppose I could," said Belinda, standing up. "But I've never done any acting. I don't suppose I'll be much good."

Miss Tyler handed her a script.

She didn't dare look at anyone else as the audition started, and her script shook in her hands. But as the scene unfolded, she concentrated on the part and imagined herself as Maggie, the malicious village girl, full of jealousy towards the beautiful Poll, until she forgot about the drama studio with Miss Tyler and her fellow pupils and only saw the country girls of all those years ago.

She lost herself so completely in her role that she came back with a start when Miss Tyler finally called out, "Cut! Thank you everyone, that was excellent. Just one more try, then we'll call it a day.

James, would you play Randolf de Vere, please? Janice, you take the part of Poll, Susi, I'd like you to play Sukey, and Belinda, could you play Rowena Saxon-Ashby?"

"But I'm not really auditioning..." began Belinda.

"You were very good as Maggie," smiled Miss Tyler. "I'm sure you could tryout as Rowena for us too?"

Belinda buried her face in the script again. She found that if she lost herself in her part, she could forget about other people's eyes upon her.

At last the audition was over and Miss Tyler collected in the scripts.

"Right, O.K. everyone. Thank you all for coming. The results of the auditions will be posted up on the drama notice board when I've made my final decisions. Probably at the end of next week."

"You were good as Maggie," said Susi, as they left the school gates. "And Rowena too. You looked and sounded like you were them."

"I nearly died of shock when Miss Tyler called me over," admitted Belinda. "I was so nervous about getting up in front of everyone, all I did was pretend I really was Maggie, or Rowena, and that made me forget I was trembling Belinda Bailey."

"Miss Tyler might give you a part. She said Maggie
Riley's a difficult part. No one else who tried that role was anything like as convincing as you. You were thoroughly nasty to poor Poll and made me feel I just wanted to curl up and die. I wouldn't be surprised if she gives it to you."

I doubt it," laughed Belinda. "She just needed someone to fill in as most people had gone home. Anyway," she said, as they reached the crossroads where their ways would part. "I'll keep my fingers crossed that you get Poll."

"Thanks," said Susie "I'll be a nervous wreck till the results come out. See you tomorrow."

The ruins of the castle towered over the village in the distance as Belinda made her way home.

Poor Poll, thought Belinda. Maggie Riley and her friends had been spiteful to her, just because she was so pretty with her long dark hair and porcelain skin. Poll had never hurt anyone, according to the story. She had always helped people in the ancient village of Castle Hedingway, with her knowledge of healing herbs.

Belinda gazed at the great castle walls and tried to imagine the proud de Vere family living there all that time ago. It wasn't Poll's fault that Randolph de Vere paid her so much attention, the story was that she tried her best to avoid him as much as she could.

But many jealous eyes watched Poll.

She wondered who would get to play Poll. Of course, all the girls wanted the starring role. She really hoped it would be Susi. She wanted the part so much.

Belinda continued through the village and came to the lake which lapped the ramparts around the castle walls, She stopped for a moment to lean against the metal railings and gazed down into the blackness of the water.

This was where they found Poll, when the ice finally thawed at the end of the long hard winter, months after that fateful Samhain Ball.

Belinda imagined the sea of flame that lit up faces and colourful dresses, as the villagers arrived for the one occasion in the year when the highest and lowest mingled, for the final celebration before the harsh frosts of winter set in.

How had Polly Miles, the loveliest girl in the village, ended her short life so dreadfully in the waters of this lake?

Belinda gazed into the blackness below her.

How cold it looked.

A light wind skimmed the surface of the lake, gently lifting her hair and undulating across the water.

So deep, so black, so cold.

A face in the glassy depths. Long dark hair fanning out and rippling across the water. Eyes closed. Scarlet spread upon the lake, a cloak stirred by the ripples and lapped by the waves.

Belinda started back away from the lake.

She wasn't wearing red.

Her uniform was grey and blue.

No scarlet.

She leaned over the railings.

There was nothing but the cold black water and her own face staring.

Belinda began to walk away. A. drunk on a bench raised a bottle of lager as she approached. Dirty trousers and tattered jacket with pockets torn.

"Tap turns on the water," he began to sing, watching her as she passed. "See the waters flow. Deep and dark and deadly. Where pretty ladies go."

Belinda shivered and hurried past, as he raised his bottle in a mockery of a toast, catching her jacket on the thorns of a bush, covered with brilliant scarlet berries that nodded in the wind as she passed.

Chapter 3

The results of the auditions were up. A crowd gathered around the drama notice board, and whoops of excitement echoed down the corridor.

Belinda sat on a nearby bench while Susi pushed her way through to find out if she'd been selected.

As Susi returned, she scanned her friend's face, hoping she had got the part of Poll she so wanted.

"Well?" she asked.

Susi sat down beside her on the bench.

"Did you get the part?"

"I didn't get Poll," said Susi. "But I did get Sukey."

"Oh, well done!" said Belinda. "Sukey's a really interesting role, much more of a character part than Poll. You'll make a brilliant Sukey."

"Yeah, a character role. I s'pose Kim's right, and I'm hardly the Beyonce of Castle Hedingway. Still, it is a good part. I did well to get it, didn't I, considering all the girls who auditioned?

"Of course, you did," said Belinda, giving her a hug. "You did brilliantly. You should be really pleased with yourself, being chosen for a major role out of all that competition. We ought to go and celebrate with a coke and doughnuts from the shop."

"Yeah," said Susi, giving her a sideways glance.

"Who has got the part of Poll?" asked Belinda. "Some bimbo, I suppose?"

"Actually," said Susi. "You have."

"But I don't understand." Belinda stared at the list on the notice board with her name at the top. She was still not convinced that it wasn't a joke. "I didn't even audition for Poll."

"Not everyone's been given the part they auditioned for," said Susi. "Miss Tyler allocates roles to the people she thinks will play them best, regardless of whether they tried for those particular ones in the auditions. An' you were good as Maggie and Rowena. She'd obviously seen enough to convince her you'll be a great lead."

"Teacher's pet!" sneered a voice in Belinda's ear.

She turned around to find Candice just behind them, whispering to Kim.

"It's not fair to give the lead to a new girl," complained Kim. "Then I s'pose Miss Tyler's only been here two years. She's not one of us from the village either. Migrants always stick together."

"I'm hardly a migrant" retorted Belinda. "London's not exactly a..."
"You're not one of us." Kim put her face close to Belinda's. "So if you know what's good for you, you'll keep away from what doesn't belong to you."

"Look, I didn't even audition for the part"
"Let's go," said Susi, pulling her away down the corridor. "Do you know why Kim's so miffed about you getting the part?"

"Because she wanted it, of course," said Belinda. "If it's going to cause so much resentment, I'd rather not bother."

"It's not that you're new, nor because she wanted to queen it over the rest of us in the starring role," said Susie "It's because Steve Winters has got the lead male as Randolf de Vere, and she can't bear the thought of another girl playing opposite him. Despite the fact he never so much as looks at her, and probably can't stand the sight of her, if he's got any taste."

"I hope it's not going to cause trouble"
"Miss Tyler chose you because you're good, so don't worry about it. Kim and Candice can whinge as much as they like. Neither of them stood a chance anyway. They haven't even been selected for a minor part. An' that's because they're rubbish. Now come on. Let's go and get those cokes and celebrate our new personas as Sukey and Poll."

"Listen..." Belinda stopped and put her hand on Susi's arm. "Susi, I hope you don't mind about me getting the part. I know how much you wanted to play Poll. I mean, I only went along to the audition to watch you."

Susi laughed. "No, don't worry about it. I was never really in the running for Poll. I'm too short and stumpy and my legs are too fat. Anyway, Sukey's a great part as well. Now, come on. Let's get those cokes."

Belinda gazed out of the science room window, ignoring the voice of the chemistry teacher.

The caretaker had a bonfire going in the grounds, heaping it with piles of dead leaves.

What will it be like to play Poll? she wondered. To step into the shoes of a girl who died mysteriously long ago? To feel as she felt, to see through her eyes?

A thick cloud of smoke uncurled from the bonfire, obscuring the figure of the caretaker. A flame leapt up to lick at the air, till it died down and was lost in a haze of grey.

Was the past like that? wondered Belinda. A bright blaze of life that flared for an instant, before sinking into the centuries like forgotten dreams?

What of Polly Miles, who had gone to the ball in her scarlet dress and cloak? And all those others who had thronged to the castle at the start of winter, continuing the tradition of

Samhain, the ancient fire festival, that heralded
the coming of the dark?

The caretaker prodded the fire again
and a million tiny red sparks flew out and
extinguished themselves on the breeze.

All those lives from the past, all those
living breathing souls who once had a form as
solid as she was now. Where were they?
wondered Belinda. Had they simply died away
on the wind, or in some strange way, did they
still breathe and dance, and sing their songs to
those who lived on?

"Hey!"
Belinda stopped and turned round. A tall,
good- looking boy with dark tousled hair came
towards her, a Liverpool bag over his shoulder
and a football tucked under one arm.

"You're Belinda Bailey, aren't you?"
"Yes?"

"Steve, Steve Winters. Congratulations
on getting the part. I thought I'd introduce
myself, seeing as we'll be acting opposite each
other. I'm playing Randolph de Vere."

"Oh, thanks, and congratulations
yourself."

"There's the bus. I'll have to shoot,"
grinned Steve, breaking into a run and turning
to wave. "See you around"

"Yeah, yeah, and thanks," Belinda
called after him.

As the bus drew off, Belinda noticed Kim Maglione, and judging by her scowl as she pressed her face against the glass, Kim had seen her talking to Steve.

Belinda carried on down the road.

So that was the famous Steve Winters, captain of the football team, heart-throb of year 10, and the starring male in the play. He looked friendly enough and it was nice of him to come over and introduce himself before rehearsals started.

But, she thought, remembering the scowling face of Kim Maglione at the back of the bus, was this play going to land her in a heap of trouble?

She took a detour home and headed down a lane until she arrived at a quiet country crossroads. A rough stone set was in the ground nearby.

Belinda stared at the stone.

Here was the place Miss Tyler had told them about in the story. This was all that marked the grave of Polly Miles.

Why had they buried her here, she wondered, in unconsecrated ground with only an unmarked stone to remind the world she had once lived and died nearby? Burials at crossroads out of town were usually reserved for suicides or witches, and Poll was neither, was she?

She dumped her bag on the grass and knelt down by the stone, placing her hands on the smooth cold surface.

She was fascinated by the story and felt the dead girl was drawing closer and closer into her life.

What had really happened that night of the Samhain ball?

Now she found herself chosen to play Poll in the school play, without even having asked.

It was almost as though some inexorable fate were drawing her into its web, and weaving together the threads of her life with those of dead Polly Miles.

What happened to you, Poll? she whispered, stroking the stone.

How did those dark waters of the lake wrap you in a cold embrace and entomb you in ice, till the springtime sun set you free - too late, and sent you floating back to the world, still in your red cloak and gown?

When she arrived home, the welcoming smell of hot steamy vegetables met her at the kitchen door. Mrs Bailey hummed to herself as she stirred the casserole.

"Polly, put the kettle on, Polly put the kettle on, Polly put the kettle on, We'll all have tea.

Hello, Belinda. Good day at school?"

"Yeah, fine thanks. Mum, why are you singing that song?"

"No reason. Just came into my head."Mrs Bailey laughed and went back to stirring the pot. "Dinner'll be ready in twenty minutes."

Belinda took off her shoes and went into the hall. She heard her mother start singing again and the words of the children's rhyme drifted towards her and followed as she climbed up the stairs.

"Sukey take it off again, Sukey take it off again, Sukey take it off again, They've all gone away."

Chapter 4

Polly hurried through the market square where tumbledown cottages teetered above rotting waste and horse dung. A fearful stench wafted from the ground, assailing her nostrils till she felt she would be sick. She took a bunch of rosemary from her herb basket and held it to her nose.

Eyes followed her. Hostile eyes, jealous eyes.

She pulled her shawl across her face.

Still she could feel those eyes upon her.

Glancing from side to side, she could see them now, peering from behind a blackened cobweb that served for a curtain at a ground floor window, leering insolently from a doorway, or glaring from beneath a hat.

She walked faster, her face averted but she could feel them boring into her still.

She stumbled over a heap of rotting cabbages. The stench made her retch. Then she picked up her skirts and ran, clutching her precious basket of herbs, through the hostile town.

Someone stood in her path. A drunk, belching over a bottle. She veered around him and carried on running, aware of his lecherous stare as she went.

Run, run. Back to her cottage. Back to the safety of stone walls and thick oak door.

Belinda sat up in bed. Strands of hair stuck clammily to her face and the palms of her hands were sticky with sweat. Her duvet was a tangled heap on the floor and the pillows were skewed halfway down the mattress.

She reached down and pulled the duvet back over her, hugging it tight. It was just a dream, she told herself. Nothing more.

But it was a dream in which she had seen through a dead girl's eyes.

The first rehearsal for the play went well, despite Kim Maglione sulking at the back with Candice, glaring if any of the girls came close to Steve.

Belinda was thoroughly engrossed in her role. Steve was fun, friendly and easy-going, and seemed quite unaware of Kim's possessive eyes watching his every move.

Finally Kim and Candice left, bored and fed-up with being ignored.

After the rehearsal, Steve said goodbye and went whistling off to get his bus. Susi and Belinda picked up their bags and began to walk to the gate.

"You know, I'd like to try and learn a bit more about this Polly Miles legend," said Belinda. "I wonder if there's anything about it in the library."

"Maybe," said Susie "We could always go and have a look. Finding more on Sukey could help me with my part. All we really know is that she was Poll's best friend and helped her with herbs and stuff."

"I wonder if there's anything that might give us a clue how she died that night," said Belinda, as they walked down the road.

Susi shrugged. "She probably just slipped and fell off the ramparts."

"She may have tripped running from Randy Randolf de Vere. But someone might've wanted her dead. Lady Rowena Saxon-Ashby? Jealous villagers? Someone who took her healing herbs for witchcraft?"

"Think you have an overactive imagination," said Susi, uncomfortably.

They came to the junction where Susi turned off. "How about we go to the library on Saturday afternoon?" said Belinda.

"If you like, though I doubt we'll find much. It's too far back in time to find out the truth. See you tomorrow."

Susi disappeared down the road and just as Belinda lost sight of her, a figure lurched from the hedge, almost stumbling into her before propping himself up against the wall.

"Sally, oh Sally," came the slurred words of his song, as the drunk Belinda had encountered by the lake lolled against the wall, a bottle of cider clutched in one hand and his battered hat slipped across one eye. "Lives down our alley..."

As she hurried past him, he pushed back his hat and stared at her with a glazed expression, swaying slightly against the wall. Then a flicker of recognition passed across his face and he raised his bottle.

"Down, down, down, down," he cried, sliding onto the pavement with his back against the wall.

"Down through the waters-oh, Where all the lovely ladies go."

Belinda shivered and hurried away.

When she reached the church, she kept her eyes averted from the graveyard The young sexton was there as usual, pretending to tend the graves as he watched her go by.

This supposedly quiet country village held more menace than the city ever did, she thought, miserably.

It was Saturday afternoon and Belinda wandered along the High Street, glancing at shop windows. She had some time to kill before she was due to meet Susie

She stopped to look at a red dress. Her vision filled with scarlet.

A girl's voice squealed across the Saturday shoppers, high-pitched, arguing with a man.

Belinda swayed and closed her eyes. She could still see scarlet. A man's face, grey and cold. High white collar and black cloth. A wooden cross jabbed at her.

"Witch!" he hissed. "Repent thy sins!"

"Belinda! "

She opened her eyes and carne back abruptly to the noisy drone of traffic and weekend shoppers to find Susi standing beside her.

"What on earth are you up to, Belinda? You looked like you were about to fall asleep on your feet."

"Oh nothing. Come on. Let's go to the library."

On their way, they had to pass the churchyard. The sexton was mowing the grass. She had thought he wouldn't be working on a Saturday. If only he wouldn't stare at her so hard every time she passed.

"What's the matter with you?" asked Susi, as they walked past the lychgate. "Your cheeks have gone bright red."

"Nothing. Just the cold," mumbled Belinda. "Let's get a move on."

"Don't tell me you get spooked by churchyards?"

"No, it's just him," said Belinda. "Back there amongst the graves. He always stares at me when I go past."

"Who?" said Susi, turning around. "I can't see anyone."

"Don't stop and look," Belinda urged.

"You must be imagining things," said Susie. "There's nobody there. Anyway, you'll always get people staring at you. Price you pay for being pretty. I don't have that problem."

Just then the sexton reappeared from behind a clump of yew, continuing to mow with his back to the girls. Susi took one look at the sturdy figure with his fair hair curling over the collar of his jacket and linked her arm through Belinda's.

"Come on, she said, glancing behind her anxiously. "Let's get going."
"What's the hurry all of a sudden?" asked Belinda, finding herself rushed along the path. "Is he following us or something?"

"No," said Susi, and bit her lip. "There's nobody there. No one at all."

In the library they found a couple of books on local folklore but neither told them anything more than they already knew about the Polly Miles story.

"This may have something," said the librarian, coming over to their table and placing an open book before them. "There's an entry here on Randolph de Vere."

"Thanks."

They quickly read down the page.

"Well," said Susi. "So it is true that Randolph pursued Poll, though he didn't seem to get anywhere."

"And he later ended up marrying Lady Rowena Saxon-Ashby," mused Belinda. "So she got what she wanted."

"There's a picture of her here," said Susi, turning the page. "She looks a stroppy, hoity-toity sort of woman."

"Maybe she pushed Polly over the battlements," suggested Belinda, leaning over to look at the page.

"Maybe," said Susie."Just look at this picture of Randy Randolf." She pointed at the page. "That curly moustache and wicked smile. Yuk! Smarmy! Arrogant too, by the look of him. He was probably used to all the girls eyeing him up, being the Lord of the manor's son and heir to the castle."

Maybe he chased Poll out to the lake when she turned him down, said Belinda. Perhaps he lost his temper..."

"and... splash! Bye bye, Poll," Susi grinned.

"There's not much in these books about Sukey," said Belinda.

Susi shrugged. "'Suppose she wasn't important enough to get a mention."

A door opened from the staffroom behind them.

"Tea up!" called a voice.

"OK," replied the librarian. "Just take the kettle off, and I'll be there in a moment."

"That's a good idea," said Susi, closing the book. "We've found all there is to find.

Let's go back into town and get ourselves a cup of tea."

"Oh there you are," said Mrs Bailey, as Belinda arrived back home. "I was just talking about you to Mrs Dale in the corner shop, telling her how you'd got the lead part in the play at school." She poured herself a coffee and sat down at the kitchen table while Belinda took her coat off. "She was very interested and told me a bit about the legend of Polly Miles."

"Oh yes?" said Belinda, kicking off her shoes and coming to sit down with her mother. "What did she say?"

"Well, apparently, you won't find it in the history books, but there's a story handed down by word of mouth that Polly Miles had been accused of witchcraft before she died.

She used herbs for healing and treated the sick, but the local rector took offence at what he called her 'pagan ways' - especially after she cured someone who was supposed to be dying. He'd read their last rites and told them their death was the will of God. He hated your Poll, apparently, and one of the rumours was that the church might have had something to do with her death."

Belinda pulled the sugar bowl towards her and toyed with it thoughtfully, remembering the images that had flashed through her mind by the dress shop earlier that day; the hostile face of the clergyman and the aggressive thrust of the cross.

Had she just been day-dreaming and allowed her imagination to run away with her, or in some strange way, was the past calling out to her and revealing some of its secrets?

That night her dreams were disturbed. She was walking down a road in pitch darkness and could see nothing. Behind her were soft voices. They were whispering about her.

But every time she looked back, there was nobody there.

Chapter 5

Belinda took out her key to get her books for next lesson.

Her locker door wasn't shut properly.

She was sure she had locked it when she went home yesterday. She pulled it open.

Belinda jumped back in disgust.

Lying on its back on top of her books, small claws clutching at air and teeth bared in a frozen snarl, was a dead rat.

She slammed the door and leaned back against the locker. She couldn't just leave the rat there and she needed her books for the lesson ahead.

Taking a deep breath, she turned around and opened the locker door again. She eased the topmost book, with the rat on top, down from the shelf, and headed for the bin.

"What're you doing?"
Startled, she almost dropped the rat on the floor.

"Aargh!" Susi screamed and jumped back against the wall.

Belinda tipped the rat into the bin.

"What the hell's going on?" frowned Susi, nervously approaching now the rat was gone.

"Someone broke into my locker and left me a present," said Belinda.

"Ugh! How horrible! It makes me feel sick! Why would anyone do that?"

Belinda retrieved her maths books from the locker. "I don't know. Some sick prank, I suppose."

"What are you going to do? Tell the teachers or something?

"No," said Belinda, relocking the door. "No one is going to scare me like that."

"But you can't just ignore it."

"Can't I?" said Belinda. "Come on, or we'll be late for maths."

Belinda chewed the end of her pen. She couldn't concentrate on geometry.

Who could have put the rat in the locker? How had it got into her locker? Did someone have a spare key? Was it someone's idea of fun?

Her stomach churned, remembering those fierce dead eyes and that bared snarl that someone meant for her.

She looked around the heads of her classmates, bowed over their maths books. Was it one of them, or a pupil from another class? Perhaps it was not one of the students. Maybe an outsider had sneaked into the school for a joke and just happened to pick on her locker. Perhaps it had not been intended specifically for her after all.

Glancing out of the window, she noticed movement by the rubbish bins outside the kitchens. Someone with his back to her was taking off the lids and rummaging around inside. At that moment one of the cooks came out with a bowl of slops and seeing the intruder, promptly chased him off with an angry wave of her hand. As he shuffled away from the bins, Belinda caught sight of his face. It was the same man she had seen drunk by the lake then again on the corner after rehearsal, who had sung her those hateful songs. Could it be just coincidence he was hanging about the grounds of the school the very morning someone had put the rat in her locker?

Kim sat frowning over the rehearsal from the back of the drama studio again. Belinda glanced at her during a break. She had never even seen Steve talking to Kim. He took as much interest in her as watching paint dry. Could it be Kim who out of spite had planted the rat in her locker? she wondered.

She had to stop thinking like that. At this rate she would be imagining half the village was responsible. It was probably just some one-off prank, and whoever had done it most likely didn't even know the locker was hers.

She got to her feet. Better to concentrate on the play.

"That's good, everyone," called Miss Tyler. "Can we try the next scene now, where Randolph comes upon Polly selling her herbs in the market square?

Susi, you don't have any lines but I'd like you to stand over there, just to the left. You're unpacking a basket, then stop when you see Randolph speak to Poll, and sneak up closer to listen to what's going on. Good.

And we want Maggie Riley and the rest of the village girls to do the same, over on the right of the stage. Ok? Maggie, make sure you really scowl at Poll. Everybody ready? Right, let's go."

"P...p... please, sir," Belinda began, as the harassed Poll. "If you have no need of my herbs, I wish you would kindly go and leave me alone."

"What?" boomed Steve, as Randolf. "Can it be that such a lovely damsel has not so much- as a tiny kiss for the Lord of the Manor's son, who would bestow the finest jewels in Christendom on upon her, if the proud little witch would but let him? Come my, dear. Just one kiss."

A loud crash came from the back of the studio.

Everyone looked round.

"Hold it there!" called Miss Tyler. "Kim! Will you watch what you're doing? If you can't manage to keep quiet, don't bother coming to watch."

Kim scowled as she picked up her bag from the floor.

"Let's take that scene again. Maggie and the girls, try and look a bit more vicious, mutter behind your hands to each other. Sukey, move closer to Poll and Randolph, that's it. Just fine."

Belinda tried not to glance at Kim and to concentrate on her lines, but as the scene progressed, and Maggie and the village girls muttered to each other behind her, she felt that the hostile eyes who watched Poll's every move, were watching Belinda too.

On her way home Belinda stared at the crumbling tower of the castle keep. A cold wind tugged her hair and she hugged her coat closer around her. A flock of rooks wheeled and cawed high above the ruin and a bank of dark cloud glowered from the sky.

She imagined Randolph de Vere, riding his horse over the drawbridge and through the castle gate and haughty Rowena, Lady Saxon-Ashby, keeping a watchful eye from the walls, while Sukey and Poll gathered herbs around the moat.

Something of all of them remained at the castle still.

The wind whipped up stronger and blew the rooks across the sky, shaking the leaves from the trees and sending a fleet of ripples skirmishing along the surface of the lake. It whistled through the ruinous turrets of the castle and hissed through the tree-tops.

As Belinda closed her eyes against the wind's sharp sting, she heard a voice calling to her through the rush of the air.

"Beware the one in midnight blue."

Belinda shielded her face from the wind but even before she looked around, she knew no one was there.

Head bowed against the wind, she went back to the main road and continued to make her way home.

She had not gone far before she heard someone call out her name. She stopped to turn round.

"Hi there," called Steve. "Don't usually see you round here."

"I sometimes come this way home, just for a change. It gets boring if you always walk the same route."

"I 'spect you must find life in Castle Hedingway pretty mind numbing after London," said Steve, hoisting his bag further onto his shoulder. "Must be great living in London. Bet you miss it, don't you?"

"Yeah," admitted Belinda, as they walked along. "Yeah, I do, but it's much better here now we've got the play.."

"She's good, Miss Tyler, isn't she. She really knows how to get the best out of people.

Hey, how d'you fancy nipping into the cafe, if you're not in any hurry to get home?"

"Hurry?" laughed Belinda. "What, to do that maths homework? Yeah, I could do with a hot drink to warm up."

"Great." Steve smiled. "Let's go."

The cafe was a short way around the corner. She sat down at a window table while Steve went up to the counter to order.

A shadow fell across the table. Someone on the pavement outside.

Through the window, she saw the drunk with his bottle of cider, tottering unsteadily. Before he could look in and see her, she snatched up the menu from between the salt and pepper pots and hid her face.

"Sorry, just say if I'm boring you? said Steve.

"What? Oh no, not at all."

"You just looked a bit... well, distracted," said Steve. "I thought maybe I was going on a bit."

"No. Look, I'm going to have to get off now. I need to catch someone before I go home." She smiled and hoisted her bag onto her shoulder. "Thanks for the drink."

"No worries. See you at school tomorrow."

Belinda scanned the street as she left but to her relief the drunk was gone.

Waving to Steve through the window, she headed for home.

"So you want to know about the Polly Miles story," said Mrs Dale, lowering her heavy frame onto a wooden chair that looked as if it would collapse beneath her any moment.

"Yes, please. My mother told me you knew something about the legend. Anything you can tell me would be useful. There's hardly any mention of her in the local history books."

Mrs Dale laughed heartily. "Dear, dear, I'm sure there ain't. Come and sit yourself down, girl. Now that's a tale as people told their children by the fireside on dark winter nights, and they grew up to tell their children after them. Passed on by word o' mouth, from generation to generation. Of course you won't find much talk o' Poll in them in them high falutin' books. It's a tale o' the common folk, if ever there was one." She laughed again then beckoned Belinda to sit down.

"Some folks reckon," she said, lowering her voice and leaning confidentially towards Belinda, "that poor Poll can't rest in peace till someone livin' finds out the truth about how she died that night.

There's some as say they've even seen her, down by the lake or round the castle walls.

Our paperboy swears he caught a glimpse of her, dressed in her long red dress and cloak an' all, her black hair flying out behind her in the wind, crying out and holding her arms to the lake. Mind you, he's a bit of a lad, that one." Mrs Dale winked. "Probably had one too many ter drink and mistook the post box for Poll's red cloak." Mrs Dale's ample bosom heaved and her chin wobbled as she laughed at her joke.

"But. . ." She grew suddenly serious and leaned forward. "When I were a girl, there were a farmer from Dunhays, sober as a judge, that one. Never touched a drop. He swore he'd seen her one night when he were looking for a cow gone astray, in a scarlet cloak, coming towards him out o' the mist by the crossroads. Quite shaken up, he were, an' though he were a big man who had no fear o' nobody livin', I tell you now, girl, he'd never go down that crossroads at night after that."

"I'm sure he wouldn't have had much to fear from Poll, if it was her ghost," said Belinda. "I don't think she'd ever harm anyone."

Mrs Dale sat back and eyed her sharply. "You know, I reckon you're right about that. But the men, see, they don't always understand like we women do. About seeing' things that they think has no business ter be there, when they've got all the business in the world. Nor about the old ways, and the healing with herbs and such.

There aren't many women left now, who knows the ancient lore, like our Poll did. But there's a few families around here still who pass things on ter their daughters, and who don't forget what's gone before."

Mrs Dale sat back in her chair and looked thoughtful for a moment. "Now, how about a nice cup o' tea? I'll put the kettle on."

The drunk was lolling across a bench near the children's playground when Polly left Mrs Dale's house to go home, his head leaning back against the top of the seat. When Belinda approached, he leaned forward and rested his hands on the knee patches of his tattered old trousers, staring at her hard.

Belinda stiffened.

Then he stood up and tottered over to the sandpit, where he picked up a stick and began to draw it across the hard wet sand.

Belinda turned away, and not wanting to walk past him, went into the nearest shop.

When she came out the drunk was gone.

Relieved, she carried on through the playground and as she passed the sandpit, she noticed the drunk had traced some words with his stick.

The letters stared from the sand like a warning. *"All are not what they seem."*

Chapter 6

Belinda arrived at school and approached her locker, noticing with relief that the door remained locked. that morning's lessons. As she took out the books she needed for the next lesson, a piece of paper fluttered to the floor. She bent down and picked it up.

Her heart sank. Someone had been in her locker again.

She looked at the sheet of notepaper in her hand. The message was cut out of newspaper.

NEW GIRLS SHOULD KNOW THEIR PLACE.
IF YOU KNOW WHAT'S GOOD FOR YOU,
DON'T TAKE WHAT'S' NOT YOURS.

She dumped it in the nearest bin.

Belinda had coffee with Susi and Steve during break.

She said nothing about the latest break-in to her locker, determined to ignore all attempts to intimidate her and to carry on as normal.

Steve was his usual cheerful, friendly self, but Susi didn't say much till he had left. Susi didn't have any close friends amongst the others, Belinda noticed. Perhaps Susi was as glad of her friendship as she was of hers.

As they made their way out of the canteen, Kim and Candice, who had been hovering by the door, stepped into their path.

"Excuse me," said Belinda coolly, staring straight into Kim's eyes.

"Excuse me," mimicked Candice.

Susi stepped back uncomfortably. "Let's wait a bit, Belinda," she said nervously.

"Stubby legs knows what's good for her," said Kim, her eyes narrowing as she firmly folded her arms in the doorway.

"You're in my way," said Belinda calmly, not taking her eyes from Kim's.

"If you know what's good for you, Bailey, you'll keep well away from Steve Winters."

Belinda stared at Kim. *If you know what's good for you...* Those were the exact words written in the note left in her locker. "What's going on here?" boomed a voice. "Kim Maglione and Candice Smith! What are you doing, obstructing the canteen entrance? Can't you see people are trying to get to lessons? Get out of the way!"

Candice and Kim stepped aside sulkily as the scowling eyebrows of Mr Jones, the Geography teacher, beetled down at them across the corridor. "What do you two think you're up to?" he snapped. "Now move aside and don't let me catch you causing trouble again."

Belinda and Susi stepped past them and headed off to their next lesson, Kim and Candice slinking behind, aware of the watchful glare of Mr Jones following them down the corridor as they went.

"You should be careful," whispered Susi anxiously. "Kim's not a good person to cross. She can make life very unpleasant, her and Candice, believe me, I know."

"You can't go through life letting people intimidate you ," said Belinda firmly. "You have to stand up to people like that. It's so stupid anyway, there's nothing between me and Steve. We're just friends. And if she didn't act so stupidly, he might take a bit more notice of her."

"S'pose," said Susi, sounding unconvinced, and she glanced furtively behind her to see where Kim and Candice had got to, then stepped closer to Belinda's side.

After the next rehearsal, another note appeared. This time it was left inside her history book after the homework had been marked.

When she picked it out of the tray, she found a sheet of the same cheap squared notepaper, pasted with black letters cut out of newsprint, slipped inside the front page.

*GIVE UP WHAT SHOULD NOT BE
YOURS - OR SOMEONE
MIGHT GET HURT.*

Belinda snatched it out of the book.

No one was going to threaten her like that. She slammed the book down on her desk.

"Belinda?" called Mrs Ball. "Is there something wrong?"

"No, Mrs Ball," said Belinda determinedly. "Nothing at all."

"Well try and put your books down a bit more quietly, can you, in future?"

Belinda heard Kim Maglione snigger behind her.

As Mrs Ball turned her back to write on the board, she firmly held the notepaper in front of her, ripped it into tiny pieces and threw it in the bin at the front of the class.

She casually walked back and sat down again at her desk. She would show Kim Maglione, and anyone else, that no one was going to intimidate her.

"You okay?" asked Susi, at break, giving her a sidelong glance as they walked towards the chocolate machine.

"Yes, I'm fine. Why shouldn't I be?"

"Oh, no reason. I just thought you looked a bit, well... distracted, that's all."

"No, I'm perfectly ok. D'you fancy coming over to my place on Saturday afternoon? We could go over our lines for the play together."

Susi slipped a coin into the machine and waited for the chocolate bar to drop through. "Sorry, I'd love to, but I've got to help my Dad out in his shop. I often give him a hand on Saturdays." There was a dull thud, and Susi lifted the metal flap to grab the chocolate bar.

"What does your Dad do?" asked Belinda, slipping in her coins.

"He owns the shoe repairer's in the village," said Susi, peeling back the wrapper. "Nothing very interesting, not like your Dad."

"I wouldn't call being a news editor especially interesting," said Belinda.

Susi wiped some chocolate from her mouth with the back of her hand. "I would. All the the latest muggings and murders dropping on your desk. And it's a bit more upmarket than a shoe repairer, just mending people's boots."

Belinda took her chocolate out of the flap. "My dad always comes home exhausted. He usually has to work really late.."

"Yeah, but it pays well, doesn't it. I wonder if I've got enough money for another bar." Susi eyed the machine again. "I mean, you've got a really lovely big modern house.

We've just got a titchy little terraced thing. I think I will have another one."

Belinda peeled off the silver paper and began to munch her chocolate as she waited for Susi.

"Ready?" she smiled, as Susi turned away from the machine and yanked the wrapper off her second bar. "Let's go."

The ruins of the castle were open to the sky.

Only the tower of the keep remained intact, though even that was crumbling in places.

Belinda walked past the gatehouse and stood in the courtyard, her hands in her pockets, looking about at the great grey walls, where many of the stones had tumbled to the ground and now lay embedded in the soft green turf.

She walked across to the keep and stopped at the foot of the ancient steps that spiralled up to the top of the tower.

This was the first time she had been inside the castle. She had only gazed on it from a distance before.

She placed her hand on the cold metal rail that the local council had put in, and read the sign on the wall at the bottom of the steps.

WARNING.
LOOSE MASONRY.

ENTER AT YOUR OWN RISK.
CASTLE HEDINGWAY DISTRICT
COUNCIL ACCEPTS NO LIABILITY.

Holding onto the rail, Belinda began to climb up the narrow passage towards the top of the tower. It was a long, steep climb and she was slightly out of breath by the time the staircase opened onto a wide stone terrace.

She found herself surrounded on all sides by a thick wall about five feet high, inset with several open slits that once had served as windows for firing arrows.

One side of the terrace had been fenced off with a rope and a large sign in red letters warned

DANGER. KEEP OUT.

Beyond the rope, a number of stones had fallen down, leaving a gaping hole in the wall.

Belinda looked down at the lake.

She could almost see the red cloak and long black hair of Polly Miles, floating like a fan across the water.

How little she really knew of Poll. Just the bare outlines of her story, handed down and garbled through the ages, some bits forgotten and lost forever.

It was so easy to imagine the ghost of poor Poll, floating along the ruins and the shores of the lake that had been her watery grave.

If she'd died suddenly, so young, thought Belinda, she too would probably want the truth to be told one day; for someone, somewhere, to know who robbed her of life; not simply to vanish from the world in a haze of mystery and doubt.

Perhaps it was too late to ever discover the truth, she thought, watching a solitary moorhen bob across the lake, but for Polly's sake, she would continue to listen to those voices which sang to her from the wind and called through her dreams, and perhaps one day she might be the one to learn what had really happened that night of the Samhain Ball, and at last set the ghost of poor Poll to rest.

Here more than ever, high above Polly's icy tomb, she felt the weight of the past pressing down upon the present, as though today was simply a fragile bubble in the fabric of time, with all those yesterdays closing in, waiting for their chance to burst through.

As she returned through the village she passed the shoemender's shop and glanced into the window. This must be Susi's father's shop. A large sign attached to the glass advertised "Keys Cut Here." Belinda went to walk on then stopped and stared at the sign.

If Susi worked there sometimes, she might be able to get hold of a key that would fit...

No. This was stupid. If she wasn't careful, she'd end up paranoid, and that was exactly what the letter writer wanted. Susi was her friend. Why should she put the rat and the notes in her locker? Besides, keys were easy for anyone to get if you knew where to go.

It could have been any one of the girls who'd give their right arm to be acting the lead in the play opposite Steve Winters. When the school football team played, it was not only Kim's eyes who watched more than the ball.

Or it could have been the drunk who hung around everywhere she went.

She sighed. She must try not to think about it, or she'd end up suspecting everyone.

But she thought, as she continued down the road, who exactly, in Castle Hedingway, could she trust?

Chapter 7

Belinda was the first one back from the gym.

"Ouch!" She pulled her hand out of her gym bag.

A drop of blood splashed onto the changing room floor and she wrapped a tissue around her finger to stop it bleeding.

She looked inside her bag, wondering what she had caught her finger on. Probably a running spike or something.

Something glinted inside.

It was a piece of broken mirror.

Scrawled across the glass in lipstick was a message.

I AM WATCHING YOU ALWAYS. GIVE UP WHAT DOES
NOT BELONG TO YOU - OR YOU WILL GET HURT.

"What's that?"

Belinda had not heard Susi come in from the pitch.

"Nothing," she said and went to drop the mirror into the wastepaper basket before the others returned from games.

It was lucky she had been the first one back to the changing rooms. She didn't want anyone else to know that someone was trying to frighten her - because they weren't going to succeed. She would just continue to ignore their stupid game.

But Susi had caught a glimpse of the red scrawl on the mirror and pulled it out of the bin.

"Oh." She stared at it in dismay then looked at Belinda. "Where did you get this from?"

"It's nothing," said Belinda. "I just found it in my gym bag."

"You've cut your finger," said Susi. "You should get a plaster for that. Look, is someone threatening you? Has there been anything else since the rat?"

"Oh, just a couple of childish notes left in my locker and in my history book," admitted Belinda reluctantly, and hearing the clatter of footsteps and the chatter of the others returning from games, she quickly took the glass out of Susi's hand and dropped it back in the bin before anyone came in.

"Aren't you going to tell one of the teachers," said Susi anxiously. "I mean, you could be in real danger. You should tell someone."

"No, said Belinda firmly, and began to get changed.

"I'm just going to ignore it. Then when the pathetic person who's doing it sees it's having no effect, they'll just have to give up."

"I wouldn't bank on that," said Susi,

doubtfully. "There're a few pretty nasty characters in this school. You don't know them like I do."

"Nasty? Moronic, more like," said Belinda, sitting down to undo her gym shoes. "It's pathetic, it really is. All because I see a lot of Steve at rehearsals. We're just friends, and even if I wanted to, I could hardly avoid him while I'm doing the play."

"Steve?" said Susi.

"Well, of course," said Belinda, crossly tugging at her shoe lace. "That's obviously what it's all about, isn't it?"

Susi frowned. "I wouldn't be too sure of that. My first thought was that it was about the play. people round here tend to be wary of newcomers at the best of times, but when they come in and manage to scoop the lead in the play, well, there's quite a few think you shouldn't have got it."

"I hadn't really thought about that," admitted Belinda. "I assumed it was over Steve. Resides, it makes no difference either way. No one is going to scare me with their silly little messages."

Susi sat down on the bench beside her. "Don't you think it might be better just to tell Miss Tyler you're busy on the night of the play, or ill or something, and not really up to it? And try and avoid Steve, just till things cool down a bit? I mean, is it really worth all this aggravation? If it was me, I'd just keep out of the limelight and let them have what they want."

"Huh, no way," said Belinda, undoing her other shoe lace. "I keep telling you, you can't go through life letting people intimidate you."

"S'pose," said Susi, doubtfully. "But aren't you worried? Just a bit? I know I would be."

"No," said Belinda firmly, yanking off her shoe. "They're too cowardly to confront me face to face. Anyway, what are they going to do? They can't really hurt me."

"I hope you're right," said Susi. "I really hope you're right."

Halloween was approaching and they now had rehearsals three times a week. The pupils making the set had worked hard and some of the scenery had already been moved into place. The costumes were nearly ready and everyone was looking forward to trying them on. The lighting people were busy trying out filters and different effects and the gantry above the stage was rigged up with spotlights and wiring.

"Right," called Miss Tyler. "We'll have a short break, then I'd like to take the scene where everyone is off stage - except Poll outside her cottage. I want to go through that long speech of yours, Belinda. Everyone else can sit down for a bit. Ok. Let's take a break."

The studio was deserted as the cast made a beeline for the drinks machine outside the canteen.

They sat swigging from cans of fizzy drink at the front of the studio as Belinda practised her speech.

Poll's soliloquy was one of the hardest parts in the play and as she went through the scene, conscious that everyone else was watching her, Belinda prayed she wouldn't forget her lines on the night. Miss Tyler made her repeat the speech several times, frowning hard, until she was satisfied.

"Good," she said at last. "Just one more time, then we'll have everyone back and go on from there."

But when Belinda was halfway through her speech, a large overhead light crashed onto the floor, missing her by inches.

"What the... " Miss Tyler ran up onto the stage. "Are you all right, Belinda?"

Belinda nodded and looked down at the heavy light which had left a gash in the floorboards.

"Who's responsible for these lights?" called Miss Tyler furiously. "David, I thought you'd checked all the lighting before we started. What's going on here? Belinda could've been seriously hurt."

A tall, thin boy with glasses came forward, scratching his head in confusion. "I did, Miss Tyler, I double checked all the lights earlier, before anyone went on stage. I always do. I can't understand it. They were all firmly bolted in place. I can't think how it came down like that. It just shouldn't have happened."

"I know it shouldn't, but it has," snapped Miss Tyler. "At least no one was hurt, but for goodness sake, make sure it doesn't happen again."

"Yes, Miss Tyler," said David, and picking up the fallen light with both hands, went off stage again, muttering to the other stage assistants.

"Right, let's get back to rehearsal," said Miss Tyler briskly. "Everyone on stage for scene four."

"Belinda," whispered Susi, when the others climbed back on the stage. "Do you think it was an accident?"

"What do you mean?"

"Well, you were alone on stage for quite a while. Was it just coincidence the light fell then? David doesn't make mistakes with the lighting. He's good at that sort of thing. Someone else could've loosened the light during the break, knowing it was your scene next. I mean, think about that message on the mirror and everything."

Belinda stared at her friend.

"Begin!" called Miss Tyler.

A few minutes into the scene, she called a halt again. "Belinda, take a break. I can see that light incident has affected you. We'll take the scene between Randolph and Rowena instead."

"Sorry, Miss Tyler," said Belinda, as she came off-stage. "I do know the lines really."

"I know you do," said Miss Tyler. "Don't worry. That accident was enough to unnerve anyone. I don't know what happened there. David is so good about checking the gantry normally. Just take a break.

And don't worry, it won't happen again."

"Belinda!"

She turned around as Steve came running up behind her when she was about to collect her coat and leave for home.

"I've lost the times Miss Tyler gave us for rehearsals next week," he said. "I wrote them down on a bit of paper and I can't find it anywhere now. Can you tell me what they were?"

Belinda, unzipped her bag and pulled out her notebook. "Here you are."

"Thanks. You're a lifesaver." Steve fumbled around in his Liverpool bag till he found a battered pad of paper, decorated with the names of Liverpool players, and jotted down the times from Belinda's pad.

"Thanks," Look, are you O.K."

"Mmm? Oh um... no, no. Sorry, I was just thinking, that's all."

"Don't think too hard, it's bad for you."

"What?"

"Thinking. It can have a detrimental effect on your health."

"Oh. Right."

"Forget it. That accident has shaken you up. You should go home. I'll see you tomorrow."

"Yeah, ok. See you then."

Belinda watched Steve walk away, carefree and whistling as he went.

Steve had no reason to want her to leave the play, had he? Or did he like Kim, or someone else, and want them to be his leading lady? No, that was ridiculous, surely? She was getting paranoid She couldn't go on suspecting everyone, especially not the few people who *were* her friends.

She hoisted her bag onto her shoulder and carried on her way, ashamed and confused.

The rough squared notepaper Steve had taken from his bag was exactly the same as that used for the warnings cut of newsprint.

Chapter 8

The final dress rehearsal arrived.

Everyone was excited to try on their costumes and act out the story in front of the newly painted set, featuring the cottages and proud towers and soaring walls of Hedingway castle, as it used to be before the centuries took their toll on the ancient stones.

Suddenly the story of Poll and the events of the past sprang vividly to life.

The highpoint of the rehearsal was the final scene at the ball where all the characters were splendidly dressed, the nobility in sumptuous gowns and cloaks, and even the poor in the very best they could muster.

When Belinda came on stage as Poll, she swept forward in a beautiful scarlet gown and a swirling cloak, her long dark waves of hair setting off the vivid red.

It was a masked ball and the black masks made by the props department, covered the top half of the face, making it difficult to work out who was who, though Poll in her brilliant scarlet stood out unmistakably from the rest.

Despite a few technical hitches, as one of the cardboard towers of the castle toppled onto Rowena's head, causing much shrieking

and hilarity, and even louder gales of laughter
when Randolph slipped on Sukey's cloak,
sending them both crashing to the floor,
overall, the dress rehearsal went well.

Miss Tyler called everyone together at
the end to go over a few last points and wished
them all "break a leg".

The cast packed up to go home in a
curious mixture of excitement and panic.

"I hope I don't forget my lines in that
long speech in scene four," said Belinda,
folding up her scarlet dress.

"You won't," said Susie "We've
practised so much we all know every line in
the play inside out by now. Even I could tell
you every word of Poll's speeches, so you
probably know them in your sleep. Anyway, if
we did get nervous on the night and go blank,
we've always got the prompt in the wings."

"Yeah, you're right," said Belinda,
giving the dress and cloak back to the
wardrobe girl. "It is nerve-racking though,
isn't it. Just the thought of all those people
who'll be out there watching us."

"You're not getting cold feet now, are
you?" asked Susi, handing over her gown and
mask.

"No. Just nervous. It's exciting though.
All these weeks of practice, from fumbling
around with the script in your hand to the final
rehearsal with costumes and stuff. And in just

a few days time, we'll be doing it in front of a real live audience."

"Yeah," said Susie "I know I'll be a bag of nerves till Saturday and Halloween. How about we go for a cake on the way home?"

"The coffee shop'll be shut by now," said Belinda.

"Tomorrow, then?"

"O.K. Our final binge before the big event."

It was late by the time Belinda arrived home.

"I've kept your dinner hot in the oven," said her mother. "How did the dress rehearsal go?"

"Not bad. Just a few technical hitches like the scenery falling down," she said, sitting down at the kitchen table. "It should be O.K. on the night though."

"Well, they say if everything goes perfectly at the dress rehearsal it means something will go wrong at the first performance," said Mrs Bailey, slipping on her oven gloves. "It's lucky to get a few things going wrong." She took out the and set it down on the table. "Right, there you are. Now, I've got to dash, or I'll be late for my keep-fit class."

Belinda took the lid off the caserole and as a delicious smelling cloud of hot steam rose up from the dish, she began to help herself to the thick welcoming stew.

"Oh, by the way," said Mrs Bailey, grabbing her bag. "I've just remembered. A letter came in the post for you this morning. I've left it up there on the sideboard. See you later."

Belinda took a mouthful of casserole then pulled the letter down from the sideboard. It was probably from Caroline or Wendy, her friends back in London.

She stared at the postmark. It had a local postmark, instead of a London stamp.

She took another mouthful of caserole and ripped open the letter.

She stopped eating, her appetite gone in a flash.

A cold sick feeling spread across the pit of her stomach.

The letters were cut out of newsprint.

THIS IS YOUR FINAL WARNING. IF YOU DO NOT LEAVE THE PLAY YOU WILL DIE, LIKE POLL.

Chapter 9

"OK," said Mrs Blakely, the chemistry teacher, to 10a. "Just write your name on the label I've given each of you and stick it onto your test tube.

Now, make quite sure you've all taken the glass stoppers out. *Don't,* whatever you do, leave the stopper in the tube. Otherwise, when the reaction takes effect, the tube will eventually explode, causing a nasty accident if anyone happens to be near. Does everybody understand?"

She paused and looked around at the nodding heads. "Good. When you've put your names on, take the test tubes over to the bench at the back and leave them in the white trays that Mr James, the lab technician has set up. Then when you've done that, you can leave them for the reaction to take place and come back after break."

Belinda removed her stopper from the test tube and smoothed on the label bearing her name. The glass was slightly damp on the outside and she had difficulty getting the label to stick, but eventually she succeeded and took the test tube to one to the back.

"You ready?" she said to Susi, who was carefully putting her test tube in the same tray.

"Yeah." "Let's go for break. I could murder a bag of crisps. But don't let me forget, I've got to go and pick up an essay from Mr Pike." They joined the noisy leaving the science lab and headed down the corridor.

"Check no one's left a stopper in, please, Sam," said Mrs Blakely to the lab technician, as she left. "I wouldn't put it past 10a to blow themselves up."

The technician grinned. "Don't worry, I'll take a look at all the experiments before I leave."

"Thanks."

As Mrs Blakely headed off to the staffroom for a much needed cup of coffee, Sam James went over to the trays full of test tubes. A few of the labels had come unstuck and he fixed them back on again, guessing as best he could which label belonged to which tube, and checked that no one had left a glass stopper. He double checked as usual then went for coffee.

Fifteen minutes later, he returned and noticing a couple of labels had fallen off again, he stuck them back on just before the flood of 10a students poured into the lab and retrieved their experiments.

"Ok, settle down now, please," called Mrs Blakely. "When you've got your test tubes back, look at page two of your worksheet and check what's happened to your experiments. Then carry out the instructions on your sheets and write down the results."

Belinda noticed her name label was askew. It had probably fallen off and someone had stuck it back on again. There was a chip on the top of the test tube. That hadn't been there before, and hers had had a small blue stain near the rim. Oh well, maybe it had got knocked, she thought. Anyway, it shouldn't make any difference to her results.

Mrs Blakely opened a window and the breeze sent Belinda's worksheet skimming across the desk and onto the floor. She went to retrieve it and just as she bent down, there was an enormous crack and a splintering of glass.

Someone screamed.

Susi was clutching her arm.

Smears of blood oozed through the white of her sleeve and trickled in a bright stream down her wrist.

Susi stared at the blood. She was pale and stunned. The students around her were all on their feet, having jumped as Susi's test tube had exploded.

Mrs Blakely rushed forward and checked the injury. "It's not too bad," she reassured Susi, who was shaking from shock. "You'll need to get it cleaned up and checked to make sure there's no glass left in the wound. Come on, let's get you down to the Nurse." She looked at Mr James who had rushed forward at the sound of the explosion. "Can you supervise the class while I'm gone, and start cleaning up this broken glass?"

"Of course."

Mrs Blakely took Susi out of the lab.

Belinda stared at the remains of Susi's experiment, lying shattered all over the floor. She noticed the rim of the broken test tube.

It had a small blue stain near the top.

With a lurch of her stomach, she realised she was looking at the remains of her original tube. The labels had been swapped.

"Ok, everyone," said Mr James. "Those of you on this bench, move away. Make sure you don't tread on any glass."

He fetched a dustpan and brush and began to sweep up the splintered fragments. Among the slivers of broken test tube, he noticed a chunk of thicker glass. He picked it up and frowned. It was the remains of a stopper. It had been left it in the test tube. But he knew he had double checked them all before he left the lab at break. He found a cardboard box and carefully slid the pieces inside.

10a were subdued, filling in their worksheets. Mrs Blakely, having left Susi with the nurse, discussed the accident with the lab technician in a low voice at the back of the room.

"You're quite sure about this?" she frowned, looking down at the shattered glass in the box.

"Totally," replied Mr James firmly. "I clearly remember checking every tube to make sure no one had left a stopper in. I double checked. There was no way that one was left in when I went for coffee. If you look at the glass around the remains of this stopper, you can see it was nowhere near the rim. Someone pushed it right into the tube so it wouldn't be noticed."

Mrs Blakely looked at the lab technician. "You mean...?"

Mr James nodded. "It looks like somebody came in during break and did it deliberately."

"Fortunately," said the Headmaster, leaning on the bench at the front of the science lab. "Susi Kettering was not badly injured. But it could have been a lot worse. Now, we know that someone appears to have come in during break and put the glass stopper in deliberately. Most likely this is someone's sick idea of a prank. But it is *not* a harmless joke." He glared around the silent class. "Someone could have been seriously hurt. I'm not going to ask you to speak out in front of everyone, but if anybody knows anything at all about this, I want them to come to me or Mrs Blakely afterwards and tell us about it. This is a very serious matter. Do I make myself clear? Good. Class dismissed."

Belinda frowned. She thought back to the warnings she had received. Should she tell the Head that she thought the tube was originally hers? Had someone deliberately put the stopper in her experiment to harm her? It was possible the plan had been foiled because the label had fallen off and got confused with Susi's.

Had the explosion of broken glass been intended to not injure Susi at all -
but her?

"No, don't say anything?" begged Susi, propping herself up on her elbow on the couch in the medical room. Her other arm was bandaged and a slight brown stain showed where some of the blood had seeped through.

"But look, someone sent me a letter through the post yesterday, warning I'd get hurt if I didn't leave the play. If the same person who sent it blocked up the test tube, it shows they really mean business."

"Oh please don't say anything," begged Susie "Look," she lowered her eyes and nervously played with the tie of her bandage. "It was my fault," she said quietly. "I must have accidentally left the stopper in when I went for break. But *please* don't tell Mrs Blakely, or the Head. It would really get me into trouble."

"But the lab technician double-checked them all."

"He must've missed mine."

"But you won't get into trouble," protested Belinda. "They're just worried it could have been worse than it was. I really think we should say something."

"No," said Susie "I don't want everyone to think I'm a total dumbo. The fuss'll all die down in a few days. *Please* don't say anything. If you're really my friend you won't."

Belinda stared at Susi. She was still pale from shock.

"What about the play tomorrow night?" Belinda glanced at the bandage. "Will you be Ok?"

"Oh yes. Don't worry. I'll be fine. The bandage won't show under the sleeves of my costume. But promise me you won't tell the Head I left the stopper in," she begged. "I just can't face getting into trouble after this. Promise me, please?"

"All right." Belinda gave in. "At least there's only one more night and the place'll be over. Perhaps things will calm down after that."

"Oh thanks!" Susi heaved a sigh of relief. "You're a real friend."

Belinda left the medical room and walked back to class.

Perhaps she was wrong not to tell the Head about everything. But Susi had looked in such a state. She didn't want to risk upsetting her even more.

Tomorrow was Halloween.

After the show, the poisonous warnings should stop.

Only a day to go.

Nothing could happen in a day - or could it?

Chapter 10

It was the evening of the play.

Belinda went early to the school, calling for Susi on the way, but found no one at home.

Never mind, she thought, looking at her watch. She probably hadn't got home yet from her stint in her father's shop.

The school was quiet and empty. No one else had arrived.

She left her bag in the changing room then went straight to Wardrobe for her costumes. Taking out the muted blue dress that she wore for most of the play, she searched the rail of costumes for the scarlet gown and cloak of the ball scene.

That was odd.

She rummaged through the clothes. It should have been next to the blue gown. Some one in Wardrobe wasn't doing their job properly. It must be here somewhere. She went again through the hanging costumes then checked in case her gown and cloak had slipped onto the floor.

They weren't there.

Her costume must be somewhere around. She would just have to wait until the students in charge of wardrobe turned up.

There was ages to go yet. Really she needn't have arrived so early.

She took the blue dress and matching shoes and headed back to the changing room.

One of the school cleaners in his checked overall was sweeping the floor and looked around as Belinda entered.

"Hello," he said, pausing to lean on his broom. "In the play are you?"

"Yes, I am."

"Oh lovely. I'll be watching meself a bit later on. I go every year. School always puts on a good show. Which part are you playing?"

"Poll"

"Ooh, I say." So I'm talking to the star."

Belinda laughed and sat down in front of the mirror.

"You're early, love. No one else here yet. There was another girl arrived straight after the school were unlocked, but it looks like she's gone again now." He stood scooped up pile of dust and dropped it into a bin bag.

"Well, I'm sure you'll make a very fine Poll.

"Will you be trying your luck with the mirror tonight?"

"What?"

"Halloween," said the cleaner. "Local tradition. You know what young girls are supposed to see in the mirror at Halloween?"

"No."

The cleaner laughed. "God love 'em! What do they teach 'em nowadays! Precious little, I reckon."

"They say that when a young girl closes her eyes and sits quiet before the mirror on the night of Halloween, if she's lucky, she'll see the face of the man she's goin' ter marry!"

Belinda laughed. "And if she's unlucky?"

"Let's hope she won't be.

Anyway, Listen to me, jabbering away when there's work ter be done." He picked up his brush and bin bag and headed for the door.

"Break a leg." You'll be a lovely Poll."

Belinda turned back to the glass. There was no need to start getting ready yet. She had arrived far too early. She had loads of time to kill.

She could always try what the cleaner said and see if she could catch a glimpse of her future husband's face in the glass.

Not that she ever intended to get married. She could think of better things to do with her life.

She sat quietly in front of the mirror. Around her was the deathly stillness of the school, its usual atmosphere of chatter and laughter shrouded in silence; as though all the children's voices of the past quivered in the air, ready to sing snatches of their songs in a quiet and listening ear.

She opened her eyes.

But she could no longer see the glass shining in front of her.

She was looking up at a clear night sky, threaded with networks of brilliant stars.

She could feel the freezing chill of the air and knew she was somewhere outside, high up.

Someone was pushing her backwards and the rough grit of stonework pressed into her spine. A hooded figure leaned closer and pushed her further over the edge of the wall.

She was going to die.

But she had to know the truth.

She had to know who, out of all her enemies, was so possessed by hatred that they would kill her.

With her last ounce of strength she managed to grab the hood of the figure who was looming over her, forcing her over the wall, nearer and nearer to the depths far below.

She pulled back the hood and saw with a shock it was a face she knew so well; the face of someone dear to her, who she trusted more than anyone else.

Then the stone pressing against her back was gone and her red cloak flapped in the wind.

The cold night air clutched at her as she fell, and only the stars looked on as death stretched out its icy fingers.

Belinda began to choke and sprang back from the mirror.

The chair crashed to the floor.

Her reflection in the glass was whitefaced and stunned.

She turned away and picked up the blue dress she had left draped across a chair and held it tightly to her.

What was happening to her? How had she seen the past through a dead girl's eyes? Whose was the face beneath the hood? Poll had been killed by someone she trusted - but whose were those treacherous eyes?

Then she heard something crackle against her chest. She looked down at the dress and tugged the zip at the back. Against the blue fabric of the lining showed a gleam of white. She pulled the dress open and found pinned to the inside a typed message on a sheet of paper. She unfastened the note and pulled it out.

ALL WARNINGS ARE AT AN END. SCARLET FLIES FROM
THE BATTLEMENTS TONIGHT - AND YOU WILL FLY
FROM HERE IF YOU KNOW WHAT IS GOOD FOR YOU.

Belinda angrily crumpled the paper in her hand.

Someone was determined to stop her playing Poll.

The note must surely mean they had taken her scarlet gown and cloak and were going to hurl them from the castle into the moat.

They weren't going to get away with it.

There was plenty of time yet to get to the castle and retrieve her scarlet dress and cloak. She tossed the crumpled ball of paper into the bin and grabbed her coat.

Hurrying towards the ruins as they towered against the night-time sky, Belinda soon reached the gate house.

She stopped and looked up at the battlements of the keep. Something scarlet flapped in the wind.

Belinda stared furiously up at the tower.

The letter writer had done exactly what they had threatened and had left her cloak flying from the battlements.

Well, she was not going to stand for that.

She ran to the keep and putting her hand on the entrance rail, looked up into the gaping stairwell.

There was no light at all and she had no torch.

The steps were steep and awkward to climb in daylight.

In the dark they were lethal.

Nevertheless, she would have to risk it, or she would never get her costume back for the play.

Taking a deep breath, she began the dark treacherous climb to the top of the tower.

Panting hard and badly shaken after a couple of frightening near misses on damp patches which had almost sent her plunging down the steps, Belinda saw the gleam of a star and knew she was finally at the top.

She stepped out onto the terrace. There was a heap on the ground. The ball gown. Streaming from the flagstaff was her scarlet cloak.

Climbing over the rope that marked off the dangerous part of the keep, she picked up the dress. Luckily it was not damaged, just a bit wet.

She looked up the cloak.

Clambering onto the ruinous wall, she managed to reach up and untie it from the flagstaff.

But just as she pulled it down, she was flung against the wall.

She caught sight of a figure dressed in jeans and a dark blue hooded jacket, before the stranger pushed her backwards across the battlements and she found herself looking up at the sky.

The words written in the sand flashed into her mind. *"Beware the one in midnight blue."*

The rough stonework pressed into her spine. Her head was forced back and high

above her she could see the brilliant
constellations in the nighttime sky.

She realised she had fallen into a trap.

Too late.

The figure loomed over her, hands on
her neck,forcing her further and further over
the wall,

Beneath the hood, an angry pair of eyes
blazed from one of the masks from the play.

Whose was the face beneath the mask?

She was going to die.

There was nothing she could do.

Forced backwards at such an angle, she
would fall over the edge and plunge through
the cold night air to her death.

But she had to know, before the end
closed in.

Whose were those glittering
treacherous eyes?

She gasped up at the stars. Then with
her last remaining ounce of strength, she
shoved her attacker and tore off the mask.

Shock made her freeze.

The face of someone she trusted.

Now she knew who had killed Polly
Miles.

A low grinding noise came from close
by. The crumbling wall of the keep gave way.

A small dark figure, clutching at a
slash of scarlet cloak, hurtled through the air to
the ground way below.

Chapter 11

"The ambulance i'll be here soon."

Steve ran towards Belinda at the lakeside. He slid his mobile back in his pocket.

"How... how did you know what had happened?" said Belinda, looking up from the edge of the reed bed.

Susi's crumpled body lay motionless in a tangle of bulrushes.

"I heard a scream as I was on my way to the play. And just as I looked over to see what the noise was, I caught a glimpse of someone falling from the tower. So I rang for an ambulance then hotfooted it round here quick."

"I hope the ambulance hurries up," said Belinda, shivering. "I wish there was something we could do."

"We've done all we can. Putting our coats over her will help keep her warm," We'd run the risk of injuring her more if we tried to move her. What the hell were you two doing up there?"

"It's a long story" I really don't want to talk about it now."

"Hey listen," said Steve, staring across the lake. "I think that's the siren now. I'll run down to the road and show them where to come."

Belinda stared down at Susi's palid face as she lay spread-eagled across the broken bullrushes, her fair hair tangled with spikes of dead leaves. Susi's closed eyelids flickered slightly and she groaned.

"Don't try to move," whispered Belinda, as Susi opened her eyes.

"You!" rasped Susi. "It should have been you!"

"Why, Susi? Why?"

"You have *everything!*" hissed Susi, through teeth clenched in pain. "Pretty face, nice house... lead in play... I wanted it so much. Should've been me! So pretty - can't keep his eyes off you... Ben, even Ben."

"Ben?" Belinda frowned in confusion. "Who's Ben?"

She wrapped her arms about herself and shivered in her thin woollen jumper. There was already a thin layer of ice glazing the surface of the water in some places and she and Steve had taken off their coats to spread over Susie.

Susi shut her eyes tight and winced with pain. "Lives next door ... works in the churchyard...best friends since... I can't remember. Did everything together... Ben and me. Even he... he asked who was my friend with the long dark hair. So pretty. Never me...

new girls shouldn't..." Susi winced again and her whole body spasmed with pain.

"Ssh" whispered Belinda. "Don't say any more."

With relief she realised Susi had lost consciousness again. She could not bear to see the contortions of pain convulsing her features, nor listen to the terrible bitterness in her voice.

She stood up and looked across the water.

Bright torches bobbed rapidly along the path beside the lake

Hurry, please hurry, she prayed silently, shivering violently as she watched the lights approach.

The paramedics gently fitted a brace around Susi's neck and lifted her onto a stretcher.

"It's OK," said one of the paramedics,, turning to Belinda. "We'll take care of her now. Luckily the reed bed cushioned the fall. If she'd landed a few feet away on the ground, or in the water, she wouldn't have stood a chance. Here, this your coat?"

Belinda nodded.

"You did well, the pair of you, to cover her up. But best put it on again quickly, love," he said, handing it back to her. "Or you'll be needing an ambulance too."

Steve and Belinda followed the stretcher to the waiting ambulance on the far side of the lake.

As the medics lifted Susi inside, she opened her eyes and stared straight at Belinda.

Belinda shuddered. A strange sensation swept through her. This was not the Susi she knew, but someone else, watching her through Susi's eyes. Then something icy snatched the injured girl's words from her lips and carried them towards her on the wind.

"I hate you, Polly Miles."

The stark white doors of the ambulance closed.

As it pulled away, the siren set up a mournful wail and cold blue light rippled over the surface of the lake, dragging the stars along the water, till the ambulance vanished and the water lay still and black once more.

"Come on."

She heard Steve's voice as he walked away, as though out of a dream, but the lake held her spellbound, drawing her into its depths and whispering its secrets.

There was no beautiful dead girl's face looking out from the cold dark water.

No mane of black hair streaming out upon the waves.

Only a deep, deep peace, as one of the secrets of the lake was finally laid to rest.

Belinda broke off a spray of scarlet berries which hung from a tree.

She let it drop into the water.

"Goodbye, Polly Miles," she whispered. "Rest in peace. I know your story at last, and mine."

A gust of wind took the berries skimming across the icy surface, then they sank and disappeared beneath the glistening brightness of the stars.

Belinda turned away from the lake and saw Steve, clutching some loose folds of fabric.

"Here," he said, holding out the scarlet cloak and gown. "You'll be needing these."

Belinda looked at them uncertainly.

"Come on," he urged, handing over her costume. "Let's get out of this cold. The play can't very well start without its two stars, can it. Miss Tyler'll be doing her nut wondering where we are. The understudy'll have to take Susi's place."

"The play? After... after all this?"

Steve smiled gently. "There's nothing more we can do for Susie." He held out his hand. "Besides, whatever happens - you know what they say - the show must go on."

Belinda took his outstretched hand and clutching her scarlet cloak and gown, she walked back with Steve towards the welcoming lights of the village.

Despite all that had gone before, the show was a great success.

Everything went perfectly.

Miss Tyler, sitting nervously in the front, having bitten her nails down to the quick before the start of the performance, was called up on stage at the end with the cast on to take one curtain call after another.

At the party afterwards, the excitement at the success of the play was interrupted by the arrival of the local police who wanted to talk to Steve and Belinda about the accident at the castle.

After they had both given statements, they returned to the party where everyone demanded to know what had happened. Belinda avoided all their questions, and Steve did his best to ward off all the curious information seekers.

"Right, that's it," he said, steering Belinda to a quiet chair in the corner and putting a coke in her hands. "No more questions."

"Thanks," said Belinda. "I really need this drink. It was so hot under all those lights.."

"It's funny, isn't it," said Steve, sitting down beside her. "That it's all over, I mean. We've been working on the show for so long, every other day after school. And now - that's it. Finished."

"Yes," mused Belinda, swilling her coke around in her glass, but as she stared at the bubbles that burst to the surface, she knew the Polly Miles story was not quite complete.

There was one more thing she had to do, for part of the mystery still remained unsolved.

Belinda rolled over to stop the alarm. She yawned and rubbed at her eyes, barely able to open them after all the events of the night before.

Still blinking she forced herself up on one elbow and looked at the time. Four o' clock in the morning. Who in their right mind would get up at such an unearthly time? On a Sunday as well, when any sane person would lounge in bed and recover from the night before.

She was tempted to just roll over and snuggle back beneath the warm cocoon of the duvet. But this was her only chance to find out the missing piece of the jigsaw.

Tomorrow would be too late.

She pushed back the duvet, climbed out of the bed and quietly began to get dressed, taking care not to wake up anyone else in the house. Then she crept downstairs, treading softly on the stairs, and put on her coat and scarf. She would need to keep as warm as she could.

It was still pitch dark as she closed the door behind her and slipped out into the night. A bright full moon shone down from a soft surround of wispy cloud and lit her way down the quiet country lane.

At the junction was a concrete bus shelter. The drunk lay fast asleep, sprawled on the hard wooden bench, mouth gaping. An empty cider bottle lay empty at his feet.

Belinda paused, staring down at the sleeping man.

He was no longer threatening to her. Nothing in Castle Hedingway held any menace for her any more. All she saw was a lonely man, lying vulnerable in the night.

She walked on. There was no traffic and no birdsong. Only the brief hoot of a barn owl flying over a field broke the stillness that lay silently over the countryside in the quiet before the dawn.

It grew misty as she left the village behind her, and when she finally arrived at the crossroads, the trees loomed like giants with outspread arms, out of the cold white haze.

Belinda crouched down to look at the stone which lay tucked among the grass, shimmering with a fine film of silvery dew in the moonlight.

How quiet and still it was here. Not a breath of wind disturbed the tranquillity of the place where Polly Miles lay finally at peace.

Belinda ran her fingers over the stone.

"Dream peacefully Polly," she whispered. "Wherever you may be. Your story is told and your truth is known."

Only one mystery still remained.

She sat down against an oak tree opposite the stone and huddled inside her coat.

She would wait..

When her eyelids flickered open again, one bright morning star remained. The full moon had already slipped away and left the sky to the rising sun.

Cold white wreaths of mist that wrapped themselves like wraiths around the trees uncoiled before her eyes

She stood up and dusted the leaves from her coat.

Ahead was the stone marking Polly's grave.

A soft shaft of morning sunlight filtered through the trees and shone gently around the stone, lighting up something left on the ground at its base.

One small posy of white and scarlet rosebuds.

Belinda looked around.

The crossroads was as deserted at dawn as it had been at night.

Nothing to show who had left the posy for Poll.

The mystery remained.

As Belinda knelt down beside the stone and gently touched the scarlet rosebuds, she remembered the closing words from the story that had started it all.

"... and although many have kept watch at the crossroads over the years, no one has ever found out just who puts the flowers on Poll Moll's grave."

Once upon a time a baby was born in a Gothic mansion in far-away Cleethorpes. The baby's parents didn't know what to call the strange little thing, which had green hair all down its back, and they were afraid it might get snatched away by goblins. They looked in all kinds of books and magazines and finally decided to call their baby Cara Louise.

The goblins never came but as she grew up in suburban Surrey, Cara Louise often saw green men in the school yard – and red, orange and blue ones too - and her bewildered parents frequently found their daughter talking to the wizard who lived in the tunnel which connected their garden to the school.

She started writing ghost stories and terrorised her younger brother with tales of hooded monks with skulls for a face and was scolded by her mother for scaring him so much that he couldn't sleep at night.

As she grew older, Cara Louise began to channel her fascination with ghoulies and ghosties and things that go bump in the night by writing mystery stories for children. She once had a proper job in the library at Southend-on-Sea but spoilt that illusion of respectability by running away to the Isle of Avalon and gained inspiration for her stories by sitting on the Glastonbury ley lines and communing with the Earth Spirit. Here she published her first book **The Boy From The**

Hills and wrote **Annie and the Dragon** in her bedroom by a window which framed Glastonbury Tor.

Cara later studied for her BA in Writing and English at the Alsager campus of Manchester Metropolitan University and - lo and behold! – her bedroom here overlooked another Hill of Power, Mow Cop in Staffordshire, which along with the nearby mysterious mansion of Biddulph Grange, served as inspiration for **The Beast of Biddersley Grange Trilogy.**

Cara Louise also has an MA in Writing For Children from King Alfred's College, Winchester. She won 2nd prizes in Writing for Children and First Three Pages of a Novel at the Annual Writers' Conference, Winchester for her archaeological thriller , BETRAYED.

She has travelled extensively, teaching English as a Foreign Language. She lived for a while in darkest Borneo, near the misty islands of the pirate-frequented Celebes Sea - until a group of armed intruders from the Sulu islands decided to ambush police officers outside one of the schools she was working in, leading to evacuation back to England.

She now lives in a small strange village on the remote North Devon coast - The land of the Zombie Apocalypse, dodging the Walking Dead.

As for her unfortunate younger brother, he still sleeps with the light on.

BY THE SAME AUTHOR

For Readers Aged 9 - 12

The Beast of Biddersley Grange

The Stones of Power

The Lords of Time

Raven Jack and the Fire of Doom

The Hounds of Darkness

Sorceress

Canis Major Mystery

The Demon's Secret

The Serpent of the Woods

Biffy and the Barrow

The Guardian and the Goddess

Annie and the Dragon

For Young Adults

Stars Upon the Ceiling

The Silent Pool

STARS UPON THE CEILING

Chapter 1

High Towers. Only the name is sure.

The large Victorian house stands way above the streets of the small estuary town of Lee-by-Sea. It overlooks the space where the great river Tamisis flows into the sea - the space between two worlds.

The twilight falls upon the darkening streets where hurrying commuters spill out of the train and make their way home from the ever spreading city, which draws relentlessly closer to their East End haven town.

The darkness closes over the oil

refineries across the water, their great
dark bulks now sprinkled with
twinkling lights, like a myriad stars
lying, scattered upon the glass of the
tide. Here at the meeting of river and
sea, city and sand, night and day,
nothing is as it seems. Nothing is stable.
Nothing is sure.

The evening breeze blows gently
in through the large dusty bay windows
and stirs the yellowing lace of the
curtains. Behind the lace the old woman
sits in her black dress and shawl. She
looks at the dark oak dresser reflectively
for a moment. Then, grasping the chair
backs for aid, she hobbles towards it.
She stoops with difficulty, wincing, with
the pain in her old bent back and opens
the cupboard. Her eyes gleam brightly
in their yellowy, wrinkled sockets as she
carefully draws out the treasure inside.

Cupping the black velvet wrapping
in wizened fingers, she shuffles back to
her seat. Gently she unwraps the velvet
and from the delicate tissue paper
within, she takes the pack of illustrated
cards in her hands.
She spreads the deck face down upon
the lace of the tablecloth and swirls
them into a star.

Stella Marison was the new girl in the sixth form of Lee-by-Sea High. She had not made many friends. Her soft southern voice set her instantly apart from the cheerful cockney of the rest of 6a who had all moved up together through the school from their earliest secondary days.

Stella tolerated school. Nothing more. But she loved to walk upon the grass-covered cliff top of Brean Head which pointed like a huge green finger into the estuary just outside the town, curving towards the jumble of Victorian houses and modern flats and shops which made up Lee-by-Sea. She would stand upon the cliffs, her long dark hair streaming out behind her in the wind, and look down at the white capped waves smashing into the hard grey rocks far below. She loved to watch the crash of water on stone, of the river into the sea.

And there she would stand, too close to the edge.

For Your Next Young Adult Book
Stars Upon The Ceiling

Go to Amazon.co.uk or Amazon.com

Printed in Great Britain
by Amazon